A PLACE IN THE
PALACE

written by Carol Reinsma
pictures by Nathan Cori

STANDARD
PUBLISHING
Cincinnati, Ohio

The Standard Publishing Company, Cincinnati, Ohio
A division of Standex International Corporation
© 1993 by The Standard Publishing Company
All rights reserved.
Printed in the United States of America.
00 99 98 97 96 95 94 93   5 4 3 2 1

ISBN 0-7847-0095-8
Cataloging-in-Publication data available

Edited by Diane Stortz
Designed by Coleen Davis

CONTENTS

LIZARD TRIES TRICKS

Lizard put on a shirt
with big flowers.
"Where are you going?"
asked Gecko.

"I am going to the palace,"
said Lizard.

"The palace walls are high.
I want to climb them."

"You need an invitation
to get inside the palace,"
said Gecko.

Lizard did not listen.

He ran to the palace.

Gecko followed him.

Lizard knocked
on the palace door.
The guard opened the door.
When he saw Lizard,
he closed the door.

Lizard sat on the step.

"I told you that you need
an invitation," said Gecko.

"Flowers should be welcome
anytime," said Lizard.

"You are a lizard
dressed like a flower,"
said Gecko.

"I will get an invitation,"
said Lizard, and he ran home.

He wrote on a white card.

"Here is my invitation,"

said Lizard.

"It won't work," said Gecko.

Lizard did not listen.

He ran back to the palace

with the white card.

Gecko followed him.

Lizard knocked

on the palace door.

The guard opened the door.

He read the card

and closed the door.

"You need a *real* invitation,"
said Gecko.

11

Lizard ran home.

He found an old party invitation.

He wrapped birthday paper
around a box.

"The guard will find out
that the box is empty,"
said Gecko.

Lizard did not listen.

He ran back to the palace
with the invitation and the box.
Gecko followed him.

Lizard knocked

on the palace door.

The guard took the invitation

and the box.

He let Lizard in.

Lizard waved his tail at Gecko.

14

Gecko cried out, "Come back!"

The door closed.

Lizard was inside the palace!

A minute later, the door opened.

Lizard rolled out,

wrapped in birthday paper.

Gecko unwrapped Lizard.

"You gave me wise advice,"

said Lizard,

"but I did not listen."

"Now will you forget

about the palace?" asked Gecko.

16

Lizard looked at the palace walls.

"No," said Lizard.

"I am going to find a way

to get a real invitation."

Listen to wisdom.
Try with all your heart to gain understanding.
Proverbs 2:2

Lizard sat on a rock.

Gecko sat next to him.

"I hear singing and laughing,"
said Lizard.

Gecko put his ear to the ground.

"I think it is coming

from the palace," he said.

Lizard sighed.

"I wish I knew a way

to get an invitation

to the palace," he said.

"Me, too," said Gecko.

Just then Turtle walked by.

He was carrying newspapers

from the palace.

"The *Palace Paper!*" cried Lizard.

"That is it!

We will read the paper.

It should tell us how

to get an invitation

to the palace."

Turtle gave them a paper.

Lizard read the front page.

Gecko read the back page.

"Listen to this!" said Lizard.

"The prince is looking for a pet.

Lizards make good pets!"

"Do you think the prince

would want me, too?"

asked Gecko.

"Two pets are better than one,"

said Lizard.

Lizard and Gecko

knocked on the palace door.

Lizard showed the guard

the newspaper.

"The prince wants a pet,"

said Lizard.

"I want to be his pet."

"Me, too," said Gecko.

"Hmm," said the guard.
"Maybe the prince will want
a lizard and a gecko."

25

Lizard and Gecko nodded.

"Yes," said Gecko.

"We will make the prince smile," said Lizard.

"Please come in," said the guard.

"Is that an invitation?" asked Lizard.

"Yes," said the guard.

26

Lizard and Gecko
walked into the palace,
arm in arm.

*The person who gets wisdom
is good to himself.
And the one who has understanding
will succeed.*
Proverbs 19:8

A BUMP AND A TUMBLE

"Wait in this room,"
said the guard.
"I will get the prince."

Lizard looked in the mirror.

"I could live here forever,"

he said.

Gecko pointed here and there.

"Look at this," he said.

"Look at that."

Lizard looked everywhere

except where he was going.

Lizard bumped into a table.

The king's checkerboard

fell to the floor.

Checkers rolled under tables.

They rolled under chairs.

"Let's get out of here fast!"

said Lizard.

Gecko saw a bowl of fruit.

"Wait," said Gecko.

"I want some fruit."

He ate grapes, cherries,

and bananas.

Lizard picked up the checkers.

"Let's go now!" said Lizard.

"One more cherry," said Gecko.

The guard came back

with the prince.

The king came, too.

"Who touched my checkers?"

asked the king.

Lizard's eyes got big

and his mouth got dry.

"Who touched my game?"

the king asked again.

Slowly Lizard stepped forward.

His tail was shaking.

The prince took Lizard's hand.

Lizard stopped shaking.

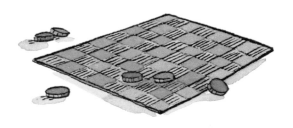

"I knocked down your checkers,"
Lizard told the king.
"I was not watching
where I was going."
"It takes a brave lizard
to tell the truth," said the king.
"I forgive you."

"May he stay?" asked the prince.

"If he plays checkers,

he may stay," said the king.

"I can learn," said Lizard.

"Good!" said the king.

"I like an honest checkers player."

Gecko stepped forward.

"I must tell the truth," he said.

"I ate all the fruit."

The king smiled and said,

"Gecko may stay, too."

*Kings are pleased
with those who speak honest words.
They value a person who speaks the truth.
Proverbs 16:13*

MUD DISHES

Lizard took a sunbath
under the skylight.
"This is the best home,"
he said.
"I like the pond," said Gecko,
"and the good food."
"I wish we could give
the king a present," said Lizard.
"What can we give him?"
asked Gecko.

Lizard walked

up and down the wall.

He thought and thought.

Gecko sat in the pond to think.

Lizard jumped down.

"We can make something

for the king," he said.

Gecko went under the water.

He came up with

a fist full of mud.

"We could make something

from mud," he said.

Lizard made his mud into a cup.

Gecko made his mud into a dish.

"These gifts are fit

for a king," said Lizard.

"Let's show them

to the prince," said Gecko.

The prince liked the cup

and the dish.

"I will put them

in the sun to dry," he said.

The cook saw the dishes

drying in the sun.

"Lizard! Gecko!" called the cook.

"Did you make these mud dishes?"

"Yes," said Lizard.

"They are gifts for the king."

"Ha, ha!" laughed the cook.

"When the king sees them,

he will throw you

out of the palace."

Lizard and Gecko

were afraid.

They tiptoed to the door.

"Lizard! Gecko!"

called the king.

"Did you make the cup

and the dish?"

Lizard shivered.

Gecko quivered.

The king held up the cup

and the dish.

"They are perfect," said the king.

"They sparkle in the sun."

Lizard and Gecko

clapped their hands.

Then Lizard said,

"This is a happy day."

Good news makes you feel better.
Your happiness will show in your eyes.
Proverbs 15:30